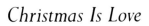

Christmas Is Love

To:
Derek
Merry First Christmas!

Love,
Papa & Gram

JOAN WALSH ANGLUND

Christmas

Is

Love

GULLIVER BOOKS

HARCOURT BRACE JOVANOVICH

San Diego   Austin   Orlando

BY JOAN WALSH ANGLUND

with loving thoughts
at Christmas

Christmas is peace
and snow so white,

Christmas is home
and candles bright.

Christmas is presents
under the tree,

Christmas is friends
and family.

Christmas is stockings
hung in a row,

Christmas is sleighbells
across the snow.

Christmas is music
in the air,

Christmas is giving,
everywhere!

Christmas is toys
and sugar plums tart,

Christmas is joy
in every heart.

Christmas is prayer
and one star above,

Christmas is children,

Christmas is love.

Requests for permission to make copies of any part of the work should be mailed to:
Permissions, Harcourt Brace Jovanovich, Publishers, Orlando, Florida 32887.

Library of Congress Cataloging-in-Publication Data
Anglund, Joan Walsh.
Christmas is love/Joan Walsh Anglund.—1st ed.
p.   cm.
"Gulliver books."
Summary: Christmas is peace and giving, sweet music
and joy; but best of all, Christmas is love.
ISBN 0-15-200425-4
1. Christmas—Juvenile poetry. 2. Children's poetry, American.
[1.Christmas—Poetry. 2. American poetry.] I. Title.
PS3551.N47C48   1988
811'.54—dc 19   87-35908

Printed and bound in Singapore by Tien Wah Press

First edition

A B C D E